SEAN TAYLOR is a children's author, storyteller and teacher. His books with Frances Lincoln include the *Purple Class* series for 7-11 year olds, *The Great Snake*, *The Grizzly Bear with the Frizzly Hair* and *Crocodiles Are the Best Animals of All!* (shortlisted for the Roald Dahl Funny Prize). For other publishers he has written *Where the Bugaboo Lives!*, *HOOT OWL: Master of Disguise* and the award-winning *When a Monster is Born* and *Robot Rumpus*. He lives partly in England and partly in Brazil.

HANNAH SHAW graduated from Brighton University with a BA in Illustration. Since then she has worked as a freelance illustrator and has written and illustrated her own stories. She currently lives in Stroud in Gloucestershire. Her books include *Evil Weasel* for Jonathan Cape, *Stan Stinky* for Scholastic, and *Crocodiles are the Best Animals of All!*, *The Grizzly Bear with the Frizzly Hair* and *Who Ate Auntie Iris?* with Sean Taylor for Frances Lincoln.

CHEDDAR

STILTON

MEXICAN SPICY

HALLOUMI

EDAM

RICOTTA

BRIE

GOAT'S CHEESE

SOFT CHEESE

HARD CHEESE

PARMESAN

For Rich – ST

In memory of Emma – HS

JANETTA OTTER-BARRY BOOKS

CRACKERS

Chutney

THE WORLD-FAMOUS CHEESE SHOP BREAK-IN

Words by

SEAN TAYLOR

Pictures by

HANNAH SHAW

Frances Lincoln
Children's Books

There it was,
between the Greengrocer's
and the Underwear Boutique.

THE CHEESE SHOP.

It was stuffed full of cheese stinkier than old socks.

The smell was yummy in our tummies!

And Daddypops said just what I knew he was going to.

"We are about to carry out the World-Famous Cheese Shop Break-In!"

"**How?**" asked my sister, Shanice.

"**EASY AS 1-2-3!**" said Daddypops.

"**All we've got to do is look natural, and walk in the front door, then that FANCY-PANTS CHEESE will be ours!**"

But it didn't work.

The next idea Daddypops had was to make a catapult and fire me in through the window.

But that didn't work either.

"**Oh dear,**" said Daddypops.

The truth was, our dad's plans for getting cheese **never** worked.

Shanice looked at him and said,

"**It maybe might be easier just to learn how to make cheese yourself.**"

I nodded.

"**Then you could open a cheese shop called FANCY-PANTS CHEESE FOR RATS!**"

FANCY-PANTS CHEESE FOR RATS!

Daddypops thought about it.

But, after a moment, his eyes lit up like he'd had the brainwave of the century.

"Rats aren't made for opening shops," he said.
"Rats are good at digging! We'll get in there by making A TUNNEL!"

PLEASE USE THE OTHER DOOR →

Next thing, he'd got a **pickaxe**
and a **shovel** and a **bucket**.
And we were digging away.

"**EASY AS PIE!**" grinned Daddypops. "You don't know how lucky you are to have a father who's clever like me!"

But, actually, it **didn't** turn out to be easy as pie.

Shanice wanted to stop because she said the tunnel was
dark and dirty and there were probably worms.

Daddypops told her not
to make a silly fuss.

MOLE

But after that a worm fell in his ear,
and he made a silly fuss himself.

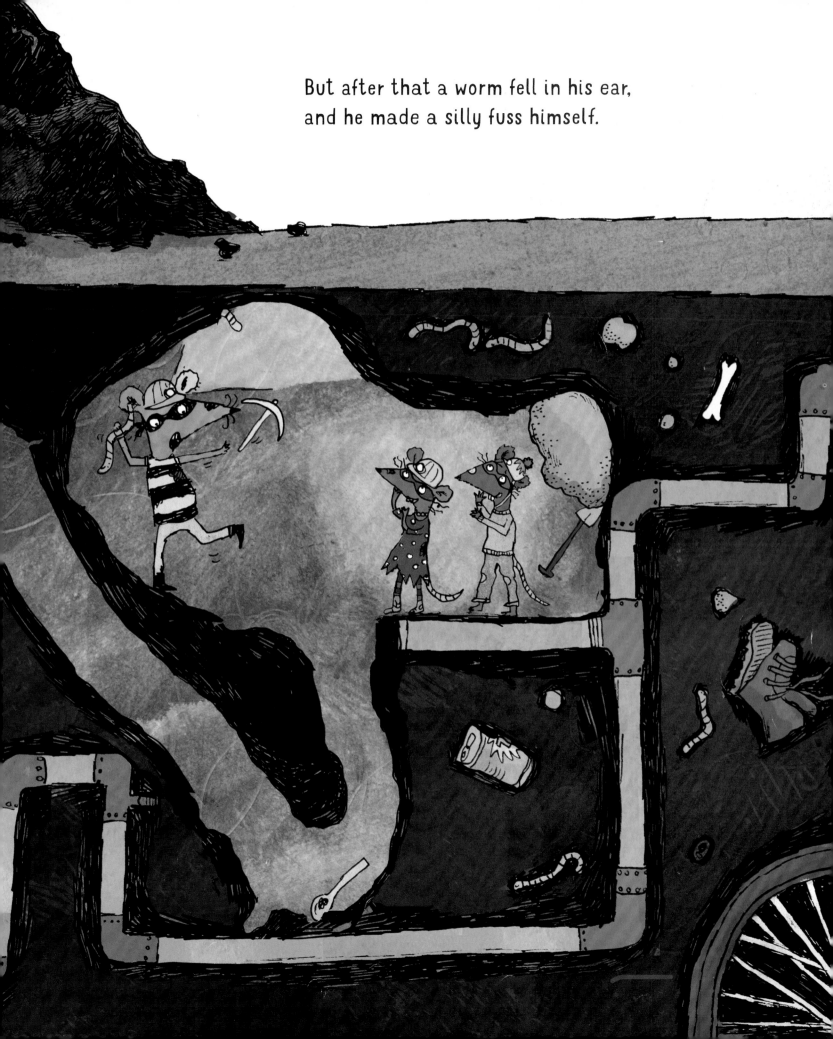

Then we got to a **very big stone.**

Daddypops managed to dig it out.

But he also tripped over
the shovel,

and dropped the stone
on his foot,

and stuck the pickaxe
through a water pipe.

And after that, we were digging up to our armpits in cold water.

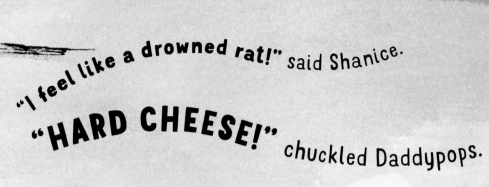

"I feel like a drowned rat!" said Shanice.

"HARD CHEESE!" chuckled Daddypops.

"It'll be worth it when we get in there. You'll see."

So we kept shovelling and shifting earth until...

But something was wrong.

It wasn't **THE CHEESE SHOP!**

We were in the Underwear Boutique.

All around us were...

pants,

bras

and
socks.

I said, "**We were probably right!
You should give up trying to steal cheese,
and learn how to make it.
Then you could open your own shop!**"

And Daddypops took us by surprise.
He looked around and he nodded.

Then he said,
"**You know what? I think I will.
I'll open my own shop!**"

And he did.

It wasn't the sort of shop we were expecting...

...but it's turned out to be a **big** success.

So now we can afford to have cheese **stinkier than old socks** EVERY DAY for breakfast!

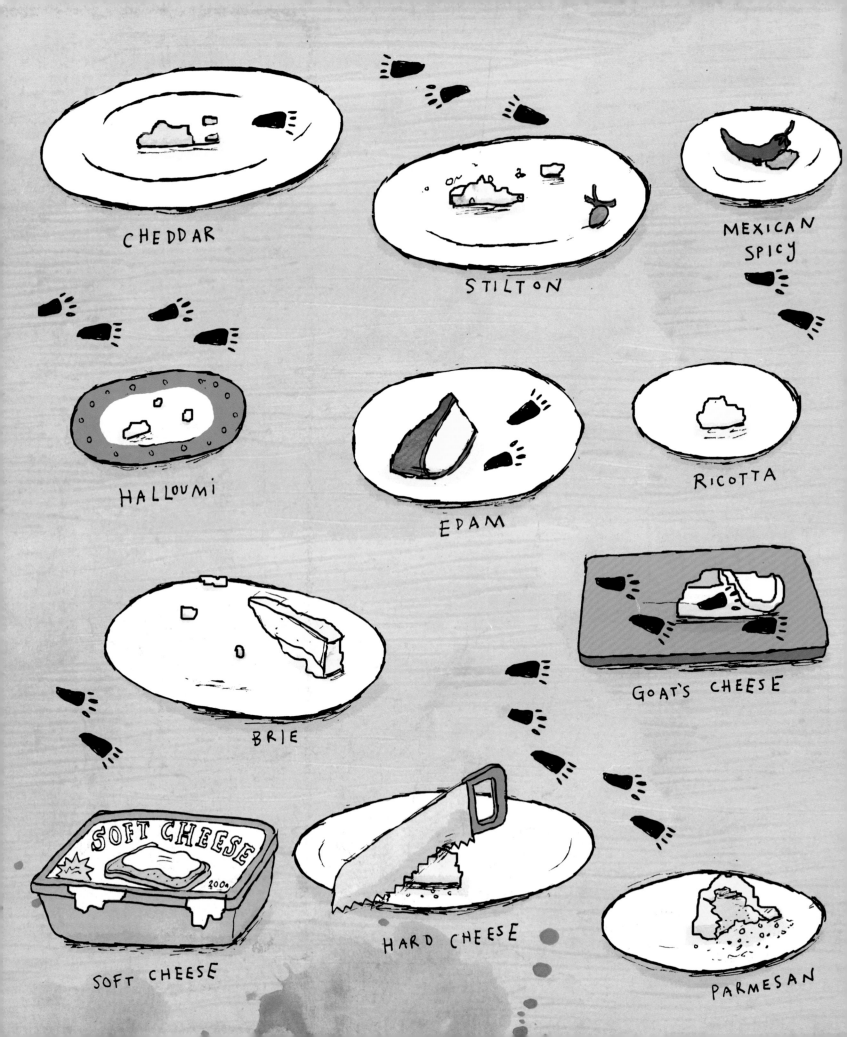

CHEDDAR

STILTON

MEXICAN SPICY

HALLOUMI

EDAM

RICOTTA

BRIE

GOAT'S CHEESE

SOFT CHEESE

SOFT CHEESE

HARD CHEESE

PARMESAN

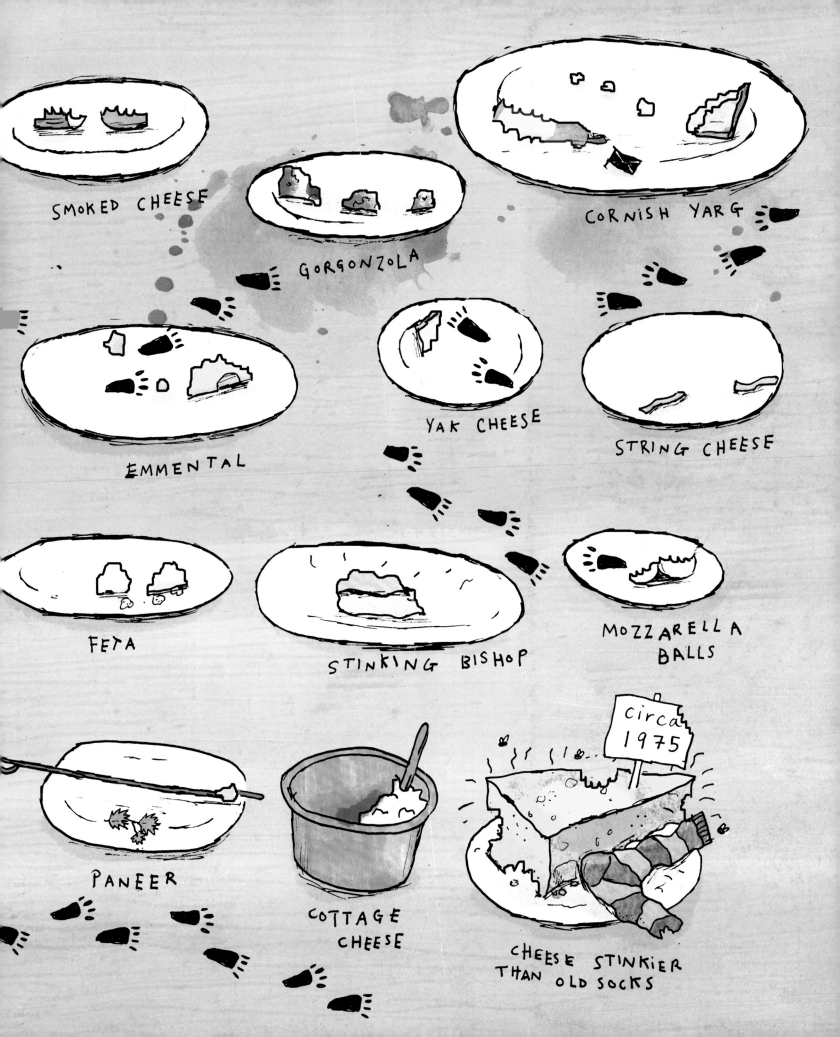

SMOKED CHEESE

GORGONZOLA

CORNISH YARG

EMMENTAL

YAK CHEESE

STRING CHEESE

FETA

STINKING BISHOP

MOZZARELLA BALLS

PANEER

COTTAGE CHEESE

circa 1975

CHEESE STINKIER THAN OLD SOCKS

MORE GREAT PICTURE BOOKS BY SEAN TAYLOR AND HANNAH SHAW FROM FRANCES LINCOLN CHILDREN'S BOOKS

We Have Lift-Off!
978-1-84780-512-6

Mr Tanner the farmer pollutes his farm and is mean to his animals. They decide enough is enough and build an intergalactic space rocket to take them up into the clean, clear skies, away from everyone who is polluting the planet. But what actually happens is far better...

'Fun and lively with a wonderful cast of animals'
Parents in Touch

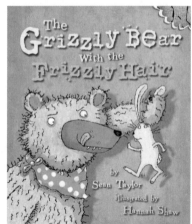

The Grizzly Bear with the Frizzly Hair
978-1-84780-144-9

The grizzly bear with the frizzly hair could frighten the feathers off a peacock. He grabs an itsy-bitsy rabbit by the ears and threatens to eat him for lunch. But the clever rabbit has an idea. By pointing out a much bigger and better meal – the bear's own reflection in the river – can he escape?

'Destined to become a read-aloud favourite'
The Bookseller

Time to Read: Who Ate Auntie Iris?
978-1-84780-478-5

One little chinchilla loves going to visit her Auntie Iris – but has to watch out for the bears on the first floor, crocodiles on the second floor and wolves on the third! Then one day, Auntie Iris goes down to put out the rubbish, and she doesn't come back. Little Chinchilla is determined to solve the mystery of her disappearance, even if it does mean talking to her scary neighbours!

Selected for Charlie Higson's best books for Christmas 2012

Frances Lincoln titles are available from all good bookshops.
You can also buy books and find out more about your favourite titles, authors and illustrators on our website: www.franceslincoln.com